The Shakespeare Collection

AS YOU LIKE IT

RETOLD BY JAN DEAN

Illustrated by Chris Mould

HODDER
Wayland

an imprint of Hodder Children's Books

 *Character list:*

Duke Senior

exiled to the Forest of Arden

Duke Frederick

brother of Duke Senior

Rosalind (Ganymede)

daughter of Duke Senior

Celia (Aliena)

daughter of Duke Frederick

Orlando

Oliver
Orlando's brother

Big Charles
Duke Frederick's wrestler

Adam
the old gardener

Silvius
shepherd

Phebe
shepherdess

5

Orlando de Boys looked around the orchard and sighed. He should be at university, or at the court, but instead he was stuck at home picking apples with Adam, the old gardener.

"It's not fair!" Orlando complained. "When my father died he didn't leave me much money, but Oliver won't even let me have that. I haven't had a penny and Oliver treats me like a servant!"

Adam nodded sympathetically. He had seen the way Oliver treated his brother. Looking up, Adam saw Oliver strut into the orchard. "*Sssh!*"

Oliver saw Orlando and stopped. "Oh, it's you," he sneered.

Something in Orlando snapped. He was sick of being treated like dirt. He grabbed Oliver by the throat.

"Let go!" Oliver gasped.

"Think of your poor dead father!" Adam cried. "Make friends for his sake!"

"Give me my inheritance!" Orlando demanded.

Oliver struggled, but Orlando held tight until Oliver agreed.

*B*ack inside the house Oliver rubbed his neck and brooded. "I'll get rid of you, Orlando," he vowed, "without handing over a penny!"

"Sir?" a nervous servant peered round the door. "Sorry to disturb you, but you've got a visitor from the court of Duke Frederick. It's Big Charles, the famous wrestler."

"Famous? From the duke? Then show him in, idiot!" ordered Oliver.

The news from court was not good. Things there had not really changed. Duke Frederick kept everything firmly under control. He had rebelled against his older brother and taken the dukedom from him. Since then Frederick ruled, while his brother, Duke Senior, lived in exile in the Forest of Arden. Duke Senior and his faithful followers camped in the woods and caves there.

"Duke Senior's camp is growing," Charles said. "Every day someone deserts Duke Frederick and joins Duke Senior in the forest..."

He hesitated, "But that's not why I'm here. I have a problem. There's wrestling at court tomorrow and I've heard that your brother, Orlando, wants to challenge me."

Oliver looked at Charles. He was a giant of a man, with muscles like Hercules'. Oliver smiled to himself. "So what's the problem?"

"Tomorrow's important to me. If Orlando fights me, I can't just fake it and let him win. But I don't want to hurt him. Talk him out of it."

Oliver's eyes glittered. Here was a way to deal with Orlando once and for all. "Charles," he said, "my brother's evil. If you fight him you'd better break his neck, because if you only hurt him he'll be back for his revenge. He'll get you, in some sneaky way – maybe poison or a trap..." Oliver pretended to choke back a tear. "It hurts me to say these things about my own brother, but it's true, Charles. It's true."

Charles was shocked. "The *rat!* If he fights me tomorrow, he'll get what he deserves."

"Oh, good," thought Oliver. "Good."

*I*n the gardens of Duke Frederick's palace his daughter, Celia, was walking with her cousin Rosalind.

"Cheer up, Rosalind."

"How can I, when my father is banished to the Forest of Arden?"

"Rosalind, I am my father's only child. One day everything will be mine. I'll share it *all* with you, I promise," said Celia.

"Ladies!" Monsieur Le Beau called. He pranced towards them, a fashion victim eager to gossip. "Oh, ladies, you *have* missed a treat!"

"What have we missed?" asked Celia.

"Such fierce wrestling! Three strong challengers fought Charles, the duke's best wrestler, and he has half-killed them all! All three have broken ribs. Come and watch the next bout."

$\mathcal{A}$s soon as Celia and Rosalind arrived at the wrestling Duke Frederick called to them. "See that young man over there? He's challenged Charles, but he's much too young to fight him. Go and persuade him to withdraw."

The young man was Orlando. Rosalind looked at him. He was *lovely*. Far too lovely to have his ribs broken.

"Don't do it," she pleaded. "We'll ask the duke to cancel the bout – then no one will say you backed out."

But Orlando stood firm. It would be better to die bravely than carry on being treated like a slave by his brother. "I must fight. It doesn't matter if I die – no one will miss me."

He wouldn't change his mind. The fight was on.

Charles swayed from side to side, like a snake about to strike. Then, with one leap, he grabbed Orlando, lifted him high off the ground and squeezed him in a bear hug. Orlando wrenched his arms free and forced back Charles' head. Grunting angrily, Charles dropped Orlando and stepped back. At once Orlando sprang to his feet and began to circle Charles.

"Isn't he *wonderful?*" Rosalind whispered.

Charles roared and charged like a bull, but Orlando was quick. He dropped into a crouch and curled up tight. Charles fell on him and then Orlando uncurled like a spring. He threw Charles across the ring – slam into the corner-post. There was a dull crack as Charles' head met the solid wood. He groaned and slumped – out cold.

The watching court cheered.

"Well done, young man!" the duke cheered. "What's your name?"

"Orlando de Boys. Sir Rowland was my father."

Duke Frederick's smile froze. Sir Rowland had been Duke Senior's trusted friend. And any friend of Senior's was an enemy to Frederick. Coldly, the duke turned away.

But Rosalind's heart beat fast. This wonderful man's father had been *her* father's dearest friend. She *must* speak to him again. As she hurried towards him she took a gold chain from round her neck. "Wear this," she said. "I have nothing else to give." Then she walked away.

Orlando gazed after her. She was the most amazing girl he had ever seen. There were hundreds of things he wanted to say to her – but his tongue felt like lead in his mouth. "What's the matter with me?" he thought. "Why can't I tell her how I feel?"

Le Beau drew him to one side. "Orlando,"
he said, "you're in danger. Today you're a hero,
but you're Sir Rowland's son, and soon Duke
Frederick will turn against you. Escape now,
while you can."

"Thanks for the warning," said Orlando.
"By the way, who was that girl?"
"Rosalind, daughter of the banished duke."

When Orlando got home, Adam met him with more bad news. Oliver was planning to kill him that very night. There was no time to lose. Scraping together the few coins they had between them, Orlando and Adam stole away.

*I*nside his palace, Duke Frederick paced the room. Meeting Orlando had disturbed him. Now he could think of nothing but enemies and treachery. When he saw Rosalind he almost snarled at her.

"Pack your bags. I want you out of here!"
"Why? What have I done?" Rosalind begged.
"Your father was my enemy."
"But, I—"
"*Father*," Celia pleaded, "don't do this. Everyone loves Rosalind, and she's like a sister to me."

"She's *too* popular," Duke Frederick hissed.
"She puts you in the shade. Once she's gone
everyone will see you shine." He turned again
to Rosalind. "You have ten days. After that –
if you come near my court – you die!"

Rosalind and Celia watched him go. They
were both stunned. Finally Celia spoke. "Well,
Rosalind, if my father has banished you, he has
banished me, too. Wherever you go, I go."

"Oh, Celia," Rosalind murmured, "where on earth can we go?"

Clever Celia smiled. "Why, if we have to leave *my* father's court, we'll go to *your* father's court. We'll go to the Forest of Arden!"

"But look at us," Rosalind protested. "Two wealthy girls – we'll be robbed before we've gone a mile."

"Then we'll disguise ourselves," Celia insisted. "I'll be a shepherdess."

Suddenly Rosalind saw how it might work. "I'm tall and slim," she said. "I'll cut my hair and dress up as a boy! I'll be your brother!"

"Called?"

"*Ganymede.* And you?"

Celia thought carefully. "We'll be strangers in the forest, so I'll have a name to suit... *Aliena.* Come on – let's do it. To Arden and adventure!"

*T*he next morning there was panic in the palace.

"Where is my daughter?" Duke Frederick raged.

One of his lords replied, "Her maid says she's gone with Rosalind. And that young man, Orlando – the one who beat Charles at the wrestling – he's missing, too..."

*R*osalind and Celia were exhausted. They had walked for hours. Now they were in the middle of nowhere, lost in a vast sea of trees and ferns.

"So *this* is the Forest of Arden," sighed Rosalind, miserably.

Just then an old shepherd came towards them.

Boldly, in keeping with her disguise as a boy, Rosalind stepped forward. "Excuse me, my name is Ganymede. My sister, Aliena, and I are looking for food and shelter. Can you help?"

The shepherd shook his head. "My master's a mean man. He never helps anyone, and anyway he's moving out. His cottage and his sheep are all for sale—"

Rosalind's face lit up. "*For sale!* That's wonderful. We'll buy the lot!"

"And if you'll be *our* shepherd," Celia smiled, "we'll raise your wages."

The shepherd was only too pleased to lead the way to the cottage.

*D*eep in the forest of Arden, Duke Senior and his faithful lords sat around a fire eating roast wild boar.

"We're better off here than in the court," Duke Senior said. "Here there are no traitors, and life is *simple* as it ought to be."

Suddenly Orlando burst forth from the undergrowth. "Food!" he demanded, brandishing his sword. "Hand it over!"

Duke Senior stared in amazement. "With pleasure," he said. "I would hate to see anyone go hungry."

Orlando was shocked by such politeness. Then he felt ashamed. "Pardon me," he begged. "You live rough in the forest – I thought you would be savages."

"Eat," said the duke.

But Orlando would not. "My old servant, Adam, is tired and starving. First I must feed him."

"Then bring him here," the duke said. "We'll take care of him. Both of you are welcome at my woodland court."

Time passed easily in the forest. Rosalind and
Celia loved living there. Back in the duke's court
there were rules about everything – rules about
clothes, rules about conversations – but in Arden
life was like a holiday. Dressed as Ganymede,
Rosalind enjoyed the freedom of the forest.

One morning, out walking, she found a poem
pinned to a tree. It was a *love* poem. A *very bad*
love poem, with awful rhymes. To her surprise,
the lady in the poem was *Rosalind*. This poem
was written about her!

Celia had found one, too. She read it aloud to Rosalind:

I will never ever find
A lovelier girl than Rosalind
I'll write her name a thousand times
I do not think
That would be wasted ink!

"Who's been littering the forest with this stuff?" Rosalind asked.

"I saw him," Celia smiled. "And he wears the gold chain you used to wear..."

31

"*Orlando!*" Rosalind blushed bright pink. They were really dreadful poems, but... *Orlando loved her!*

"Sssh! There he is," Celia whispered.

"No need to shush, *Aliena.* I'm *Ganymede,* so I'll speak to him." Then she strode through the ferns towards Orlando. "Nice day."

Orlando sat on a tree stump and sighed.

"What's wrong?" Rosalind asked.

"I'm in love," replied Orlando.

"No. Lovers look sleepless and pale. They wear odd socks and forget to comb their hair. You look fine. You're not in love," teased Rosalind.

"I am. Totally," insisted Orlando. "I'm sick with it."

"I'll cure you."

"How?" asked Orlando.

"I'll pretend to be this Rosalind person and you can pour your heart out to me. I'll soon put you off being in love!"

To Celia's amazement, Orlando agreed. Rosalind had completely fooled him. Now Celia watched as Orlando went down on his knees and spoke of his love. Little did he know that the 'boy' pretending to be Rosalind really *was* Rosalind!

After Orlando had gone, Rosalind lay in the ferns and stared at the sky. *Orlando loved her!* He'd told her such wonderful things. But he thought he was talking to a boy... it was all getting very confusing! As she lay there, she heard voices. She sat up and looked around. A handsome shepherd was running after a pretty shepherdess.

"Phebe! Come back. *I love you!*"

She ignored him.

"Please, Phebe!"

"Get lost, Silvius!" snapped the shepherdess.

Rosalind, so happy to be in love, felt sorry for poor Silvius. "Be nice to him!" she called.

Phebe, startled, looked around. "And who are you?"

"Ganymede."

"Mmm, very nice, too," Phebe whispered to herself.

"Marry me, Phebe," Silvius pleaded.

"Yes, marry him!" Rosalind urged.

Phebe tossed her head. Never mind Silvius – Ganymede was a much better catch...

$\mathcal{R}$osalind was cross. Orlando was late again. He had promised to meet Ganymede for the next part of his cure for love-sickness. Where could he be?

"*Ganymede!*"

Rosalind looked up expectantly, but it was not Orlando, it was Silvius. He had a letter.

"It's from Phebe. She's written to tell you off for interfering between us the other day. I think she hates you," Silvius said.

Rosalind opened the letter. Oh dear... It was full of Phebe's love for Ganymede. Rosalind handed the letter to Silvius. "Look, Silvius," she said. "Phebe says she loves me and would do anything for me. So tell her this: I want her to marry you. OK? Now, on your way. It seems we have a visitor."

Celia was gazing up into the eyes of a tall, dark man.

"Is this Ganymede's cottage?" he asked.

Celia nodded and fluttered her eyelashes.

"I have a message from Orlando," he said. "He's hurt, but he will be here when his wound is bandaged."

"*Hurt?*" Rosalind began to panic.

"He's fine. I'm his brother, Oliver. I was searching for him in the forest when I was attacked by a lion. Orlando fought the beast and saved my life, even though I've been a rotten brother and really didn't deserve it..."

"I'm glad he saved you," Celia whispered.

Rosalind looked at Oliver and Celia. Love had struck them like lightning. It seemed that in the forest of Arden you could catch love like the flu!

Still disguised as Ganymede and Aliena, the two girls went with Oliver to see Orlando. To Rosalind's dismay, Phebe was there – and so was Silvius.

"Marry me, Phebe," Silvius moaned.

"Marry me, Ganymede," Phebe cried.

Rosalind looked down at her boy's clothes and groaned. What a mess her disguise had led her into. "Phebe," she said, "I promise that if ever I marry a woman, it will be you. Now, *you* make *me* a promise."

"Anything!" said Phebe.

"If I ask you to marry me and you say 'no', then you must marry Silvius."

Phebe laughed. She would never say 'no' to Ganymede.

Then Ganymede made an announcement. "Oliver, you will marry Aliena. Orlando, you will marry Rosalind. Silvius, you will marry Phebe. All of this will happen tomorrow at Duke Senior's camp right here in Arden."

*I*t was a golden morning, full of sunshine and birdsong. In Duke Senior's camp a crowd had gathered to witness these amazing weddings. Orlando and Oliver were there, Phebe was there with Silvius. Duke Senior waited to see if this Ganymede boy he'd heard of could really deliver all he'd promised.

Then, slowly, through the forest came a procession.

"A parade!" exclaimed Duke Senior.

There was a handsome forester wearing golden robes acting the part of Hymen, the god of marriage. Behind him walked two lovely women dressed in white.

The small one lifted her veil.

"Aliena!" cried Oliver.

"No," said Duke Senior. "She is my niece, Celia!"

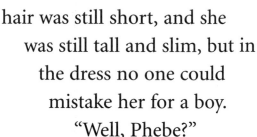

Then Rosalind lifted her veil. Her hair was still short, and she was still tall and slim, but in the dress no one could mistake her for a boy.

"Well, Phebe?" Rosalind asked.

"If I asked you to marry me now, what would you say?"

"*Ganymede?*" Phebe clapped her hand to her mouth as she realized the truth.

Duke Senior and Orlando stared wide-eyed at the beautiful woman before them.

"*Rosalind?*" they said, together.

Rosalind smiled at their surprise and looked around. It was like a miracle. She had found her father *and* a husband, all in this magical forest.

Music played and the couples were married, just as Ganymede had predicted.

While everyone celebrated a rider galloped in.

"Duke Senior," he cried, "your brother, Frederick, came to the forest to murder you. But on the way he met a holy man who stopped him in his tracks and made him think about his life. He is a changed man. Now he has given up the dukedom and become a monk..."

Could this be true? It seemed anything was possible in the Forest of Arden.

"The court is yours!" the messenger continued. "Return and rule!"

"Now everything is perfect," said Rosalind. "Orlando and Oliver are true brothers, and Frederick has given back what he stole. And everyone who fell in love has found their proper partner."

Then a country band began another song and the whole of Arden was filled with music.

The Shakespeare Collection

Look out for these other titles in the Shakespeare Collection:

Richard III Retold by James Riordan
Richard, Duke of Gloucester, is a ruthless, ambitious man with
only one thing on his mind – he's determined to become King
of England. Richard will stop at nothing to secure his destiny,
not even cold-blooded murder. Can anyone stand in his way?

King Lear Retold by Anthony Masters
King Lear has set his daughters a test to prove how much they
love him. Goneril and Regan flatter the old king, but his
youngest daughter, Cordelia, loves him too much to play the
game. In a moment of anger, Lear banishes Cordelia. Can any
good come out of this rash decision?

Julius Caesar Retold by Kathy Elgin
Julius Caesar is the leader of Rome, but the power has gone to
his head. Even his best friend, Brutus, can see that this tyrant
has to be stopped for the good of the people. When Brutus finds
himself involved in a plot with Cassius to kill Caesar, he wonders
if any good can come from a murder...

You can buy all these books from your local bookseller, or order
them direct from the publisher. For more information about
The Shakespeare Collection, write to: *The Sales Department,
Hodder Children's Books, a division of Hodder Headline Limited,
338 Euston Road, London NW1 3BH.*